THE ADVENTURES OF MIMI AND MOTO THE MOTORCYCLE MONKEYS

BY NANCY GERLOFF AND MARK AUGUSTYN

ILLUSTRATED BY ESTEBAN ALVARADO

LITTLE RIDER ENTERPRISES

THIS IS
MIMI and MOTO!
THE MONKEYS WHO LOVE MOTORCYCLES.

SOMETIMES THEY RIDE
MOTORCYCLES IN THE DIRT.

SOMETIMES THEY RIDE
MOTORCYCLES TO THE BEACH!

MOTO LIKES
TO RIDE WHEN IT IS
DIRTY AND MUDDY.

MIMI LIKES
TO RIDE WHEN IT IS WARM AND SUNNY.

MIMI AND MOTO ALWAYS
BOOTS AND GLOVES THAT

WHEN THEY RIDE MOTORCY

THEY ARE VERY HARD TO (

MOST OF ALL, MIMI AND MOTO LOVE TO RIDE TOGETHER.

WHEN THEY GO TO SLEEP, MOTORCYCLE ADVENTURES

MI AND MOTO DREAM OF OREVER AND EVER.

THE END

THE ADVENTURES OF MIMI AND MOTO THE MOTORCYCLE MONKEYS

Printed in China.
First U.S. edition 2016
ISBN 978-0-692-73534-3

Published by
Little Rider Enterprises

www.mimiandmoto.com